© for the French edition: 2018, Cambourakis
Titel of the original edition: *Au 10, Rue des Jardins.*
Recettes du monde à partager
© for the English edition: 2019, 4th edition 2023,
Prestel Verlag, Munich · London · New York
A member of Penguin Random House Verlagsgruppe GmbH
Neumarkter Strasse 28 · 81673 Munich

This edition was published by arrangement with
The Picture Book Agency, France. All rights reserved.

Library of Congress Control Number: 2018965319

Project management: Melanie Schöni
Copyediting: John Son
Production management: Susanne Hermann
Hand lettering: Felicita Sala
Printing and binding: DZS Grafik, Slovenia
Paper: Magno Natural

Prestel Publishing compensates the CO_2 emissions produced
from the making of this book by supporting a reforestation
project in Brazil. Find further information on the project here:
www.ClimatePartner.com/14044-1912-1001

Penguin Random House Verlagsgruppe FSC® N001967

Printed in Slovenia

ISBN 978-3-7913-7397-3
www.prestel.com

WHAT'S COOKING AT 10 GARDEN STREET?

Felicita Sala

PRESTEL

MUNICH · LONDON · NEW YORK

FOR MY MOTHER, WHOSE DOOR IS ALWAYS OPEN,
WHOSE TABLE IS ALWAYS FULL.
                              — F.S.

SOMETHING SMELLS GOOD
AT N. 10, GARDEN STREET.
DELICIOUS, ACTUALLY!

IN THIS KITCHEN,
PILAR BLENDS UP
TOMATOES IN A BIG POT

2 POUNDS RIPE TOMATOES

1-2 GARLIC CLOVES, MINCED

1 TSP SALT

huile D'OLIVE EX

8 OUNCES OF YESTERDAY'S BREAD, CHOPPED

½ CUP EXTRA VIRGIN OLIVE OIL

SERRANO HAM

2 HARD BOILED EGGS

SALMOREJO

CHOP THE TOMATOES AND BLEND IN A LARGE BOWL OR POT WITH THE MINCED GARLIC UNTIL SMOOTH. PASS THROUGH A SIEVE TO GET RID OF SEEDS. ADD THE BREAD AND BLEND UNTIL SMOOTH. MIX IN THE SALT AND OLIVE OIL. SERVE WITH CHOPPED HARD BOILED EGGS AND STRIPS OF SERRANO HAM.

SERVES 6

NEXT DOOR, MISTER PING
STIR FRIES SOME BROCCOLI.
HIS NEPHEW BENJAMIN CALLS
THEM LITTLE TREES.

2 SMALL HEADS OF
BROCCOLI, CHOPPED

1 TBSP
SESAME
OIL
+ more
for
frying

SALT

1 TBSP
SESAME
SEEDS

1 TBSP
MINCED
GINGER

Sesame oil

香油

2 TBSP SOY SAUCE

½ CUP
Water
or STOCK

LITTLE TREES
(SESAME SOY BROCCOLI)

TOAST SESAME SEEDS IN A HOT, DRY PAN UNTIL THEY START TO POP.
IN A CUP, MAKE THE SAUCE BY MIXING SESAME OIL, SOY SAUCE, AND
WATER. HEAT A LARGE WOK OVER MEDIUM HEAT, ADD A LITTLE
SESAME OIL AND STIR FRY THE GINGER FOR 1 MINUTE. TURN HEAT
TO HIGH AND STIR FRY BROCCOLI FOR 2 MINUTES. ADD THE SAUCE
AND STIR FRY FOR 5-6 MORE MINUTES. STIR IN THE SESAME SEEDS
AND SEASON WITH SALT.

SERVES 4

ACROSS THE HALL, MARIA MASHES
AVOCADOS WITH A FORK.

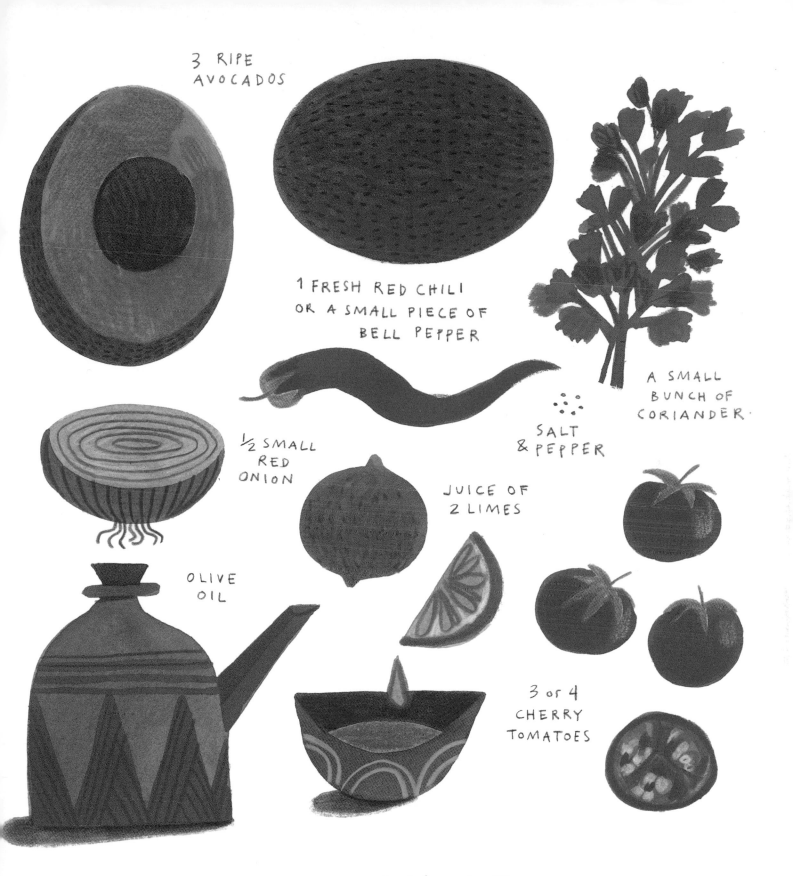

3 RIPE
AVOCADOS

1 FRESH RED CHILI
OR A SMALL PIECE OF
BELL PEPPER

A SMALL
BUNCH OF
CORIANDER

SALT
& PEPPER

½ SMALL
RED
ONION

JUICE OF
2 LIMES

OLIVE
OIL

3 or 4
CHERRY
TOMATOES

GUACAMOLE

MASH THE PULP OF 3 AVOCADOS. FINELY CHOP THE TOMATOES, CHILI,
RED ONION, AND CORIANDER. ADD TO THE AVOCADOS ALONG WITH
THE LIME JUICE, A FEW DROPS OF OLIVE OIL, SALT AND PEPPER.
SERVE WITH NACHO CHIPS.

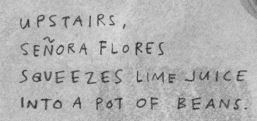

UPSTAIRS,
SEÑORA FLORES
SQUEEZES LIME JUICE
INTO A POT OF BEANS.

2 GARLIC CLOVES, MINCED

1 TSP GROUND CUMIN

1 RED ONION

½ GREEN BELL PEPPER

JUICE OF 2 LIMES

3 CANS OF BLACK BEANS, (OR 1½ POUNDS COOKED + DRAINED)

1 TBSP TOMATO PASTE

1 TSP DRIED OREGANO

2¼ CUPS STOCK (OR BEAN COOKING LIQUID)

4 STRIPS OF BACON, CHOPPED

BLACK BEAN SOUP

FINELY CHOP ONION AND BELL PEPPER. HEAT UP A LARGE POT, ADD SOME OLIVE OIL AND FRY BACON FOR 2 MINS, UNTIL BROWN. ADD ONION AND BELL PEPPER AND COOK ON GENTLE HEAT FOR 5 MINS. NOW ADD THE GARLIC, CUMIN, OREGANO, AND TOMATO PASTE. STIR AND COOK ANOTHER MINUTE. ADD THE BEANS AND STOCK AND SEASON WITH SALT. SIMMER FOR ½ HOUR, STIRRING OCCASIONALLY. ADD LIME JUICE AT THE END AND SERVE WITH RICE AND SOME CORIANDER (OPTIONAL).

SERVES 4-6

MISTER MELVILLE THINKS
ABOUT THE BEST ANGLE
TO CUT INTO HIS FISH.

4 FILLETS OF LEMON SOLE
(OR OTHER WHITE FISH),
SKIN REMOVED

4 TBSP BUTTER

2 TBSP OLIVE OIL

LEMON JUICE

SALT + PEPPER

4 TBSP FLOUR

PARSLEY

A HANDFUL OF PINENUTS

SOLE MEUNIÈRE

TOSS THE FILLETS IN THE FLOUR AND SHAKE OFF EXCESS. HEAT
BUTTER AND OLIVE OIL IN A LARGE FRYING PAN. ADD FISH AND COOK
FOR 2 MINUTES UNTIL GOLDEN. TURN FISH AND SEASON WITH SALT
AND PEPPER. ADD PINENUTS AND COOK FOR ANOTHER 2 MINUTES.
ADD LEMON JUICE AND SOME CHOPPED PARSLEY, STIR THE PAN
A LITTLE AND SERVE.

SERVES 4

IN ANOTHER KITCHEN, SIGNORA LELLA
TASTES HER FAMOUS SAUCE, DECIDING
IT NEEDS MORE SALT.

1 PACKAGE OF SPAGHETTI

4 TBSP OLIVE OIL

2 SHALLOTS

BASIL

SALT

1 CLOVE OF GARLIC

PARMESAN

25 OUNCES OF STRAINED TOMATOES

SPAGHETTI al POMODORO

IN A POT, HEAT OLIVE OIL AND GENTLY COOK THE FINELY DICED SHALLOTS AND THE WHOLE GARLIC CLOVE FOR 3-4 MINUTES. ADD THE STRAINED TOMATOES AND TURN UP THE HEAT FOR 2 MINUTES. ADD ½ CUP OF WATER AND SOME SALT, COVER THE POT AND COOK ON VERY LOW HEAT FOR AT LEAST 1 HOUR, STIRRING OCCASIONALLY. ADD SOME BASIL LEAVES IN THE LAST 10 MINUTES. WHEN THE SAUCE IS ALMOST DONE, ADD THE SPAGHETTI TO A LARGE POT OF BOILING, SALTED WATER. WHEN COOKED, DRAIN THE SPAGHETTI AND ADD TO THE POT OF SAUCE, STIRRING ON HIGH HEAT FOR 1 MINUTE. SERVE WITH GRATED PARMESAN AND SOME BASIL LEAVES.   SERVES 4-5

UP ON THE THIRD FLOOR,
MISTER SINGH OPENS
A CAN OF COCONUT MILK.

2 CUPS RED SPLIT LENTILS

1 TSP TURMERIC

2 TBSP CURRY POWDER

3 TBSP COCONUT OIL OR GHEE

1 CAN of COCONUT MILK

4 CUPS WATER

1 TBSP GRATED GINGER

2 CARROTS

1 CLOVE of GARLIC, MINCED

SUNSHINE COCO

3 TBSP TOMATO PASTE

2 TSP SALT

4 GREEN ONIONS

COCONUT DAHL

FINELY CHOP THE CARROTS AND GREEN ONIONS. GENTLY COOK THE VEGETABLES IN A LARGE POT WITH THE OIL/GHEE AND A PINCH OF SALT. ADD THE GINGER, GARLIC, TURMERIC, AND CURRY POWDER. STIR FOR 1 MINUTE, THEN ADD THE TOMATO PASTE WITH A LITTLE WATER AND STIR SOME MORE. ADD THE LENTILS AND WATER AND SIMMER FOR 20 MINUTES. ADD THE COCONUT MILK AND SALT AND SIMMER FOR ANOTHER 15 MINUTES, STIRRING OCCASIONALLY AND ADDING A LITTLE WATER IF NEEDED. SERVE WITH RICE. SERVES 6/8.

MEANWHILE,
MRS GREENPEA DELIGHTS
IN THE GOLDEN CRUST
OF HER MINI QUICHES.

3 EGGS

3 SHEETS OF SHORTCRUST PASTRY, CUT INTO 24 CIRCLES, ABOUT 4 INCHES IN DIAMETER

1 CUP BACON (OR LARDONS), CUT INTO SMALL STRIPS OR PIECES

1½ CUP RICOTTA

1 CUP HEAVY CREAM

½ CUP GRUYÈRE, GRATED

A PINCH OF GRATED NUTMEG

1 LEEK

MINI - QUICHES

PREHEAT OVEN TO 350°F. FRY BACON UNTIL CRISPY, REMOVE FROM PAN, LEAVING 1 TBSP OF FAT IN PAN. AFTER REMOVING DARK LEAVES FROM THE LEEK, CUT IN HALF LENGTHWISE AND RINSE WELL. THEN SLICE THINLY CROSSWISE AND COOK GENTLY IN BACON FAT UNTIL SOFT. SET ASIDE TO COOL. IN A LARGE BOWL, COMBINE THE RICOTTA, HEAVY CREAM, EGGS + CHEESE WITH A PINCH OF SALT AND NUTMEG. MIX IN BACON AND LEEK. PLACE 12 PASTRY CIRCLES IN A 12-CUP MUFFIN TRAY AND FILL WITH 2-3 TSP OF FILLING. BAKE FOR 15-20 MINS AND REPEAT WITH THE SECOND BATCH.

MAKES 24

JOSEF AND RAFIK TAKE THE JOB
OF ROLLING VERY SERIOUSLY.

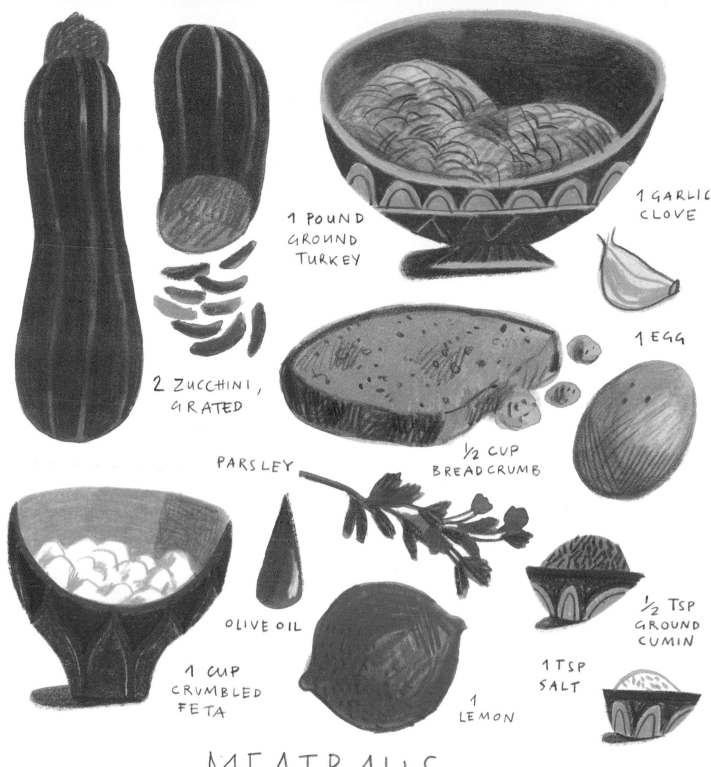

1 POUND GROUND TURKEY

1 GARLIC CLOVE

2 ZUCCHINI, GRATED

1 EGG

½ CUP BREADCRUMB

PARSLEY

OLIVE OIL

1 CUP CRUMBLED FETA

1 LEMON

½ TSP GROUND CUMIN

1 TSP SALT

MEATBALLS
(with turkey, zucchini & feta)

PREHEAT OVEN TO 400°F. IN A PAN, COOK THE ZUCCHINI WITH A LITTLE OIL AND A PINCH OF SALT UNTIL SOFT. SOFTEN THE BREAD CRUMB WITH MILK OR WATER AND SQUEEZE OUT EXCESS LIQUID. MINCE THE GARLIC AND FINELY CHOP THE PARSLEY. PLACE THE GROUND TURKEY IN A LARGE BOWL AND ADD THE ZUCCHINI, BREAD CRUMBS, GARLIC, PARSLEY, CUMIN, SALT, EGG, FETA, AND THE ZEST OF 1 LEMON. MIX WELL WITH YOUR HANDS, THEN MAKE SPOON-SIZED BALLS. HEAT UP A LARGE PAN AND FRY THE MEATBALLS WITH SOME OLIVE OIL UNTIL GOLDEN BROWN (5 MINUTES). PLACE IN A ROASTING PAN LINED WITH PARCHMENT PAPER AND BAKE FOR 6-7 MINUTES UNTIL COOKED. SERVE WITH A LITTLE LEMON JUICE.

MISS ISHIDA
QUIETLY REACHES
FOR A BOTTLE OF MIRIN.

2 BONELESS, SKINLESS CHICKEN THIGHS

3 TBSP SOY SAUCE

1/2 CUP DASHI OR CHICKEN STOCK

3 TBSP MIRIN

MIRIN みりん

3 SHALLOTS

2 EGGS

2 TBSP SUGAR

2 CUPS COOKED RICE

1 GREEN ONION

OYAKODON
(chicken & egg rice)

IN A BOWL, MIX TOGETHER THE DASHI OR STOCK, MIRIN, SOY SAUCE, AND SUGAR. THINLY SLICE THE SHALLOTS AND CUT CHICKEN INTO BITE-SIZED PIECES. PLACE SHALLOTS AND DASHI MIX IN A SMALL PAN AND BRING TO A BOIL. ADD CHICKEN, LOWER HEAT TO MEDIUM-LOW AND COOK FOR 6 MINUTES. LIGHTLY BEAT THE EGGS AND POUR OVER THE CHICKEN, STIRRING GENTLY FOR 30 SECONDS. TURN OFF THE HEAT, COVER, AND LEAVE TO REST FOR A COUPLE OF MINUTES. SERVE OVER FLUFFY RICE WITH SOME SLICED GREEN ONIONS ON TOP (OPTIONAL). MAKE THIS DISH IN SMALL BATCHES OF 1 OR 2.   SERVES 2

IN ANOTHER APARTMENT,
MISTER IBRAHIM
REMEMBERS HIS CHILDHOOD
HOME AND SMILES.

3 MEDIUM EGGPLANTS

2 CLOVES of GARLIC, MINCED

3 TBSP OLIVE OIL

1/2 TSP SALT

CHOPPED PARSLEY

TAHINI F

3 TBSP TAHINI

1/2 TSP SMOKED PAPRIKA

3 TBSP LEMON JUICE

BABA GANOUSH

PREHEAT OVEN GRILL TO 400°F. ROAST WHOLE EGGPLANTS ON A BAKING DISH FOR 1 HOUR, UNTIL SOFT INSIDE. ONCE COOL, SCOOP OUT THE FLESH INTO A BOWL. MASH WITH A FORK OR PUREE WITH AN IMMERSION BLENDER. MIX IN TAHINI, MINCED GARLIC, LEMON JUICE, PAPRIKA, SALT, PARSLEY, AND OLIVE OIL. BLEND UNTIL SMOOTH.
SERVE WITH PITA BREAD OR CARROT STICKS.

AS THEY REACH FOR YET ANOTHER
OLIVE, PENELOPE AND MILES
BELIEVE THEY'RE THE ONES
WHO ARE COOKING.

1 CUP
WHITE
RICE

2 POUNDS
SPINACH

1 CUP WATER

JUICE OF
HALF A LEMON

2 RED
ONIONS

1 CUP PITTED GREEK OLIVES

3 GARLIC
CLOVES

1 CUP
FETA

Kalamata
OLIVES

GREEN RICE

FINELY CHOP ONIONS AND SAUTÉ IN A LARGE POT WITH OLIVE OIL
AND A PINCH OF SALT UNTIL GOLDEN (ABOUT 10 MINS). MINCE THE
GARLIC AND ADD TO THE POT ALONG WITH THE RICE AND TOAST FOR
1 MINUTE. ADD SPINACH IN PARTS UNTIL ALL IS WILTED. ADD WATER
AND 1 TSP OF SALT, COVER AND COOK ON LOW HEAT FOR 15 MINUTES.
IF NECESSARY, ADD WATER TOWARD THE END AND STIR. WHEN THE RICE
IS COOKED, ADD CRUMBLED FETA, CHOPPED OLIVES + LEMON JUICE.

SERVES 4-6

UP ON THE FIFTH FLOOR, JEREMIAH CANNOT SEEM TO REMEMBER THE WORDS TO HIS FAVOURITE SONG.

1/3 CUP CRUNCHY PEANUT BUTTER

1 STICK SOFTENED BUTTER

1/2 TSP SALT

1/2 TSP BAKING SODA

1 TSP VANILLA

1¼ CUPS FLOUR

2/3 CUP CHOCOLATE

1 EGG

1/2 CUP BROWN SUGAR

flowr

PEANUT BUTTER + CHOC CHIP COOKIES

BEAT TOGETHER THE BUTTER, PEANUT BUTTER, AND VANILLA UNTIL FLUFFY. BEAT IN THE EGG. ADD SUGAR, FLOUR, SALT + BAKING SODA. CHOP THE CHOCOLATE INTO SMALL CHIPS AND ADD TO THE MIX. WITH YOUR HANDS, MIX THE DOUGH ON A LIGHTLY FLOURED SURFACE. ROLL DOUGH INTO A LOG SHAPE, ABOUT 2 INCHES IN DIAMETER. WRAP IN CLING WRAP AND REFRIGERATE FOR 2 HOURS. PREHEAT OVEN TO 350°F. CUT THE LOG INTO ½ INCH ROUNDS AND BAKE ON A TRAY FOR 15 MINNTES UNTIL GOLDEN BUT STILL SOFT.

JEMIMA AND ROSIE ARGUE
OVER WHO TOOK THE LAST
BANANA.

2 OR 3 RIPE BANANAS

¾ CUP BROWN SUGAR

1 STICK BUTTER

2 TSP BAKING POWDER + ½ TSP SALT

VANILLA

2 EGGS

½ CUP YOGURT

1 CUP BLUEBERRIES

1½ CUPS FLOUR

BANANA & BLUEBERRY BREAD

PREHEAT OVEN TO 350°F. BUTTER AND FLOUR A LOAF PAN. IN A BOWL, MIX BUTTER, EGGS, AND SUGAR. ADD BANANAS AND MASH WITH A FORK. ADD YOGURT. ADD FLOUR WITH BAKING POWDER AND SALT AND MIX WELL. LIGHTLY COAT THE BLUEBERRIES IN FLOUR AND GENTLY FOLD THEM INTO THE MIX. POUR BATTER IN THE LOAF PAN AND BAKE 45-50 MINUTES.

SMELLING THE FIRST
STRAWBERRIES OF THE YEAR,
MATILDA DREAMS ABOUT
THE SUMMER THAT WILL COME.

2 PINTS OF
STRAWBERRIES

1 TBSP
LEMON
JUICE

2 CUPS
FLOUR

CRÈME FRAÎCHE
TO SERVE

½ CUP
SLIVERED
ALMONDS

½ CUP BROWN
SUGAR

Crème Fraîc

1 STICK BUTTER

STRAWBERRY CRUMBLE

PREHEAT OVEN TO 350°F. CUT STRAWBERRIES IN HALF AND PLACE IN A
SMALL OVEN TIN WITH LEMON JUICE AND A SPOONFUL OF SUGAR. CUT BUTTER
INTO SMALL CUBES AND MIX WITH FLOUR AND SUGAR IN A BOWL. RUB
THE MIXTURE WITH YOUR FINGERS UNTIL YOU HAVE A CRUMBLY MIX,
LIKE WET SAND. COVER STRAWBERRIES WITH THE CRUMBLE AND PAT DOWN.
SPRINKLE ALMONDS ON TOP. BAKE 40 MINUTES UNTIL GOLDEN. SERVE
WARM WITH CRÈME FRAÎCHE OR VANILLA ICE CREAM.

EVERYTHING IS READY.
IT'S TIME TO GO
DOWNSTAIRS.

PULL UP A CHAIR
AND GRAB A PLATE!
EVERYBODY'S WELCOME
AT 10 GARDEN STREET.